The Three Bears' Christmas

by **Kathy Duval**

illustrated by **Paul Meisel**

Holiday House / New York

To my parents, Tom and Gloria, who introduced me to The Three Bears,
and to Glen, Jon Paul, and Kara, my greatest gifts
Thanks to Erin, Kelly, Ginny, Peggy, Sydnie, and Carmen for your incredible help
K. D.

To Mary, Claire, Regina and all the wonderful people at Holiday House
P. M.

Text copyright © 2005 by Kathy Duval
Illustrations copyright © 2005 by Paul Meisel
All Rights Reserved
Printed in the United States of America
www.holidayhouse.com
First Edition
1 3 5 7 9 10 8 6 4 2
Library of Congress Cataloging-in-Publication Data
Duval, Kathy.
The Three Bears' Christmas / by Kathy Duval ; illustrated by Paul Meisel.— 1st ed.
p. cm.
Summary: After taking a walk on Christmas Eve while their freshly baked gingerbread cools,
Papa, Mama, and Baby Bear arrive home to encounter another "trespasser" who does not have
golden hair but wears a red suit and leaves presents.
ISBN 0-8234-1871-5 (hardcover)
[1. Bears—Fiction. 2. Santa Claus—Fiction. 3. Christmas—Fiction.] I. Meisel, Paul, ill. II. Title.
PZ7.D9547Th 2005
[E]—dc22
2003067646
ISBN-13: 978-0-8234-1871-8
ISBN-10: 0-8234-1871-5

It was Christmas Eve.

Baby Bear hung bells on the Christmas tree.

Papa Bear hung stockings
on the mantel.

Mama Bear baked three gingerbread bears. One was for
Papa, one was for Mama, and one was for Baby Bear.
"May I have my gingerbread?" asked Baby Bear.
"It's too hot," said Mama. "You'll need to wait."

"But I'm hungry now!" said Baby Bear.
"Let's take a walk," said Papa. "That will help you wait."

On their walk, the bears played What Do I See?
Papa saw a rabbit. Mama saw the Big Dipper.
"I see something flying over the moon," said Baby Bear.
"It must be a shooting star," said Papa.

Then the bears played What Do I Hear?
Papa heard an owl.

Mama heard pinecones falling.

"I hear bells," said Baby Bear.
"It must be icicles," said Mama.

"Look!" said Baby Bear. "Someone opened our door!"
"It must have been the wind," said Papa and Mama.
The three bears headed for the kitchen.

"Someone nibbled my gingerbread!" said Papa.

"Someone nibbled my gingerbread too!" said Mama.

"Someone gobbled my gingerbread all up,"
said Baby Bear, "and left a woolly mitten!"

The bears followed a trail of crumbs.
"Someone is messy," said Mama.
"Someone sat in my chair!" said Papa.
"Someone sat in my chair too!" said Mama.

"Someone big broke my chair," said Baby Bear, "and dropped a fuzzy hat!"

The bears saw boots on the stairs.

"Someone has tired feet," said Papa.

Papa, Mama, and Baby Bear rushed upstairs.

"Someone rumpled my bed!" said Papa.
"Someone rumpled my bed too," said Mama.
"Someone in a big hurry rumpled my bed,"
said Baby Bear, "and forgot a red coat!"

Jingle, jingle, jingle.
"Someone is ringing bells!" said Papa, Mama,
and Baby Bear.

They ran downstairs.

"Someone left presents under the tree!" said Papa.

"Someone filled
our stockings too!"
said Mama.

"Ho, ho, ho!"

"Someone jolly!" shouted Baby Bear, "and there he is!"

"Merry Christmas, Santa!"